To Bubs and Goose and pigeons everywhere! – A. C.

For Wilfred – R. W.

PIGEON
MATH

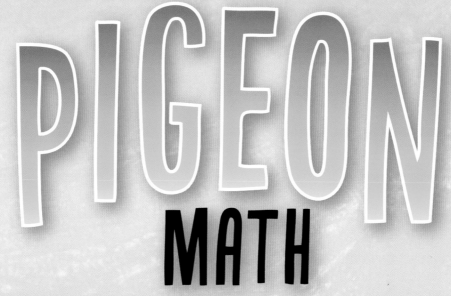

BY ASIA CITRO

ILLUSTRATED BY RICHARD WATSON

One bright and sunny morning, ten pigeons...

...four.

As I was saying, one bright and sunny morning, FOUR pigeons...

Oh, bother.

...seven. Where were we?
Oh, right. One bright and sunny, um,
afternoon, SEVEN pigeons and one cat...

More pigeons? This seems like a bad idea.

But OK...seven plus two is...

...nine. One (gulp) bright and sunny afternoon, NINE pigeons and ONE CAT!

Wait a minute. What are they doing?

MINUS ONE CAT!

One bright and sunny (and, er, slightly windy) afternoon, NINE clever pigeons and ZERO cats...

NOOOOOOOOOOOOOOOOO!

Yes, I see that you are very funny.
But it's no use.

It's practically pigeon bedtime!

Oh. You do make a good point.
I suppose I could at least END the story.

In that case...um...three plus seven is...

...ten. One warm and sparkly evening, TEN pigeons snuggled together after a particularly busy day...

...and went to sleep.

THE END!!!!!!

Oh, gosh. Sorry!

Library of Congress Control Number: 2019900120
ISBN 9781943147625

Text copyright © 2019 by Asia Citro
Illustrations copyright © 2019 by The Innovation Press
Illustrations by Richard Watson

Published by The Innovation Press
1001 4th Avenue, Suite 3200, Seattle, WA 98154
www.theinnovationpress.com

Printed and bound by Worzalla
Production date June 2019

Cover lettering by Nicole LaRue
Cover art by Richard Watson
Book layout by Tim Martyn